W9-BFS-907

ZOO-MATE WANTED

Korrie Leer

Albert Whitman & Company
Chicago, Illinois

Leah and Lilly had two things in common:

they shared a room, and
they loved the zoo.
Besides that...

the two sisters couldn't be more different.

Leah's

Lilly's

Leah's
Lilly's

Leah's

Lilly's

And some days, that made living together really hard.

So Lilly packed her bags. “I never wanted to *live* in a zoo!” she yelled. “In fact, only a zoo animal could handle a roommate as wild as you!”

"That's a great idea!" Leah shouted back. "I'll find a new zoo animal roommate! A ZOO-MATE!"

It didn't take very long for someone new to slither through the door.

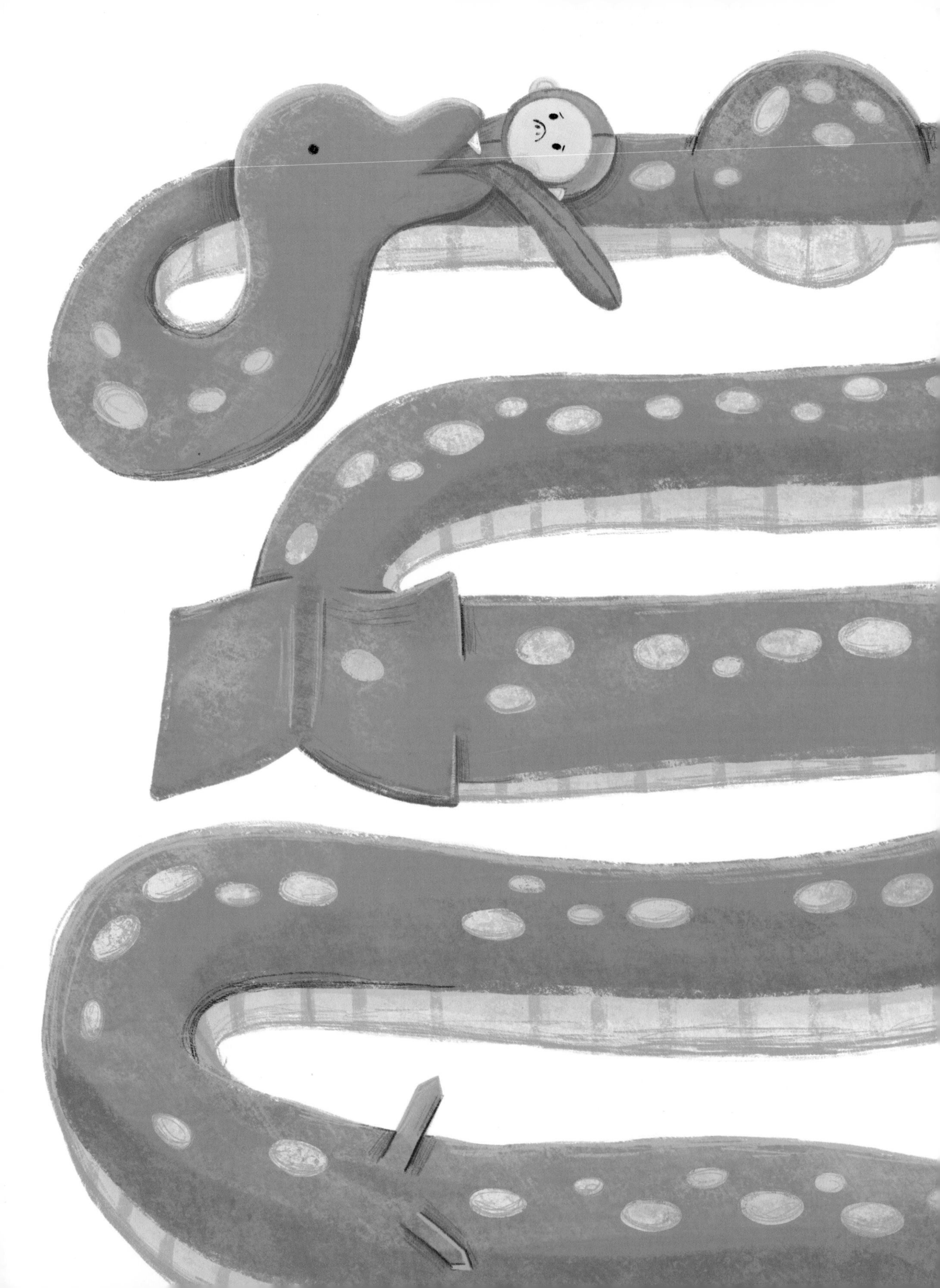

Things went well until snack time.

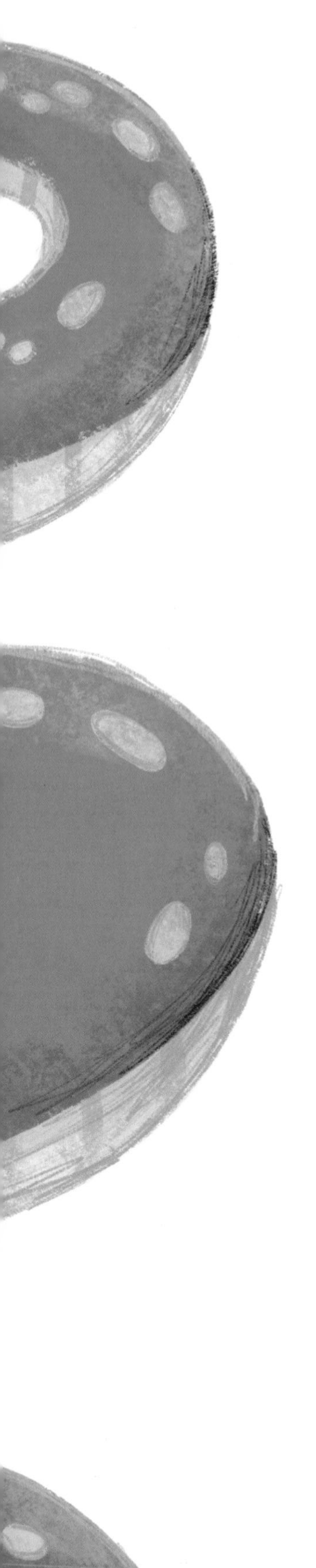

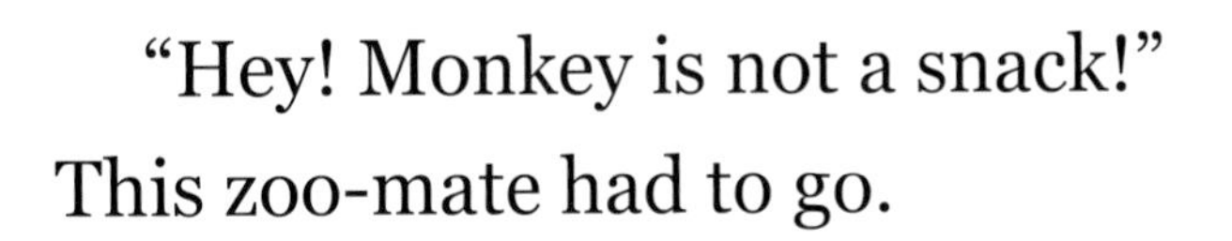

“Hey! Monkey is not a snack!”
This zoo-mate had to go.

The next zoo-mate was a little bouncier.

She could paint all of the places
Leah could not reach.

But Leah quickly learned why staying on the paper was important.

"Nope!

Nope!

Nope!"

Any zoo-mate who painted on Monkey was not right! She kicked the kangaroo out.

The next zoo-mate was an obvious "N-n-n-o thanks."

Monkey didn't like the cold...and neither did Leah.

Finally, Leah found someone who fit in just right with her and Monkey.

Lemur knew how to have fun!

But things went too far, even for Leah. No amount of fun was worth putting Monkey in danger.

"ABSOLUTELY NOT."

Leah sighed. Maybe she wasn't wild enough to handle living with an animal.

But that didn't mean that her perfect zoo-mate wasn't still out there.

Leah made some changes.

Zoo-Mate Wanted

She hoped the right zoo-mate would see her new flyer.

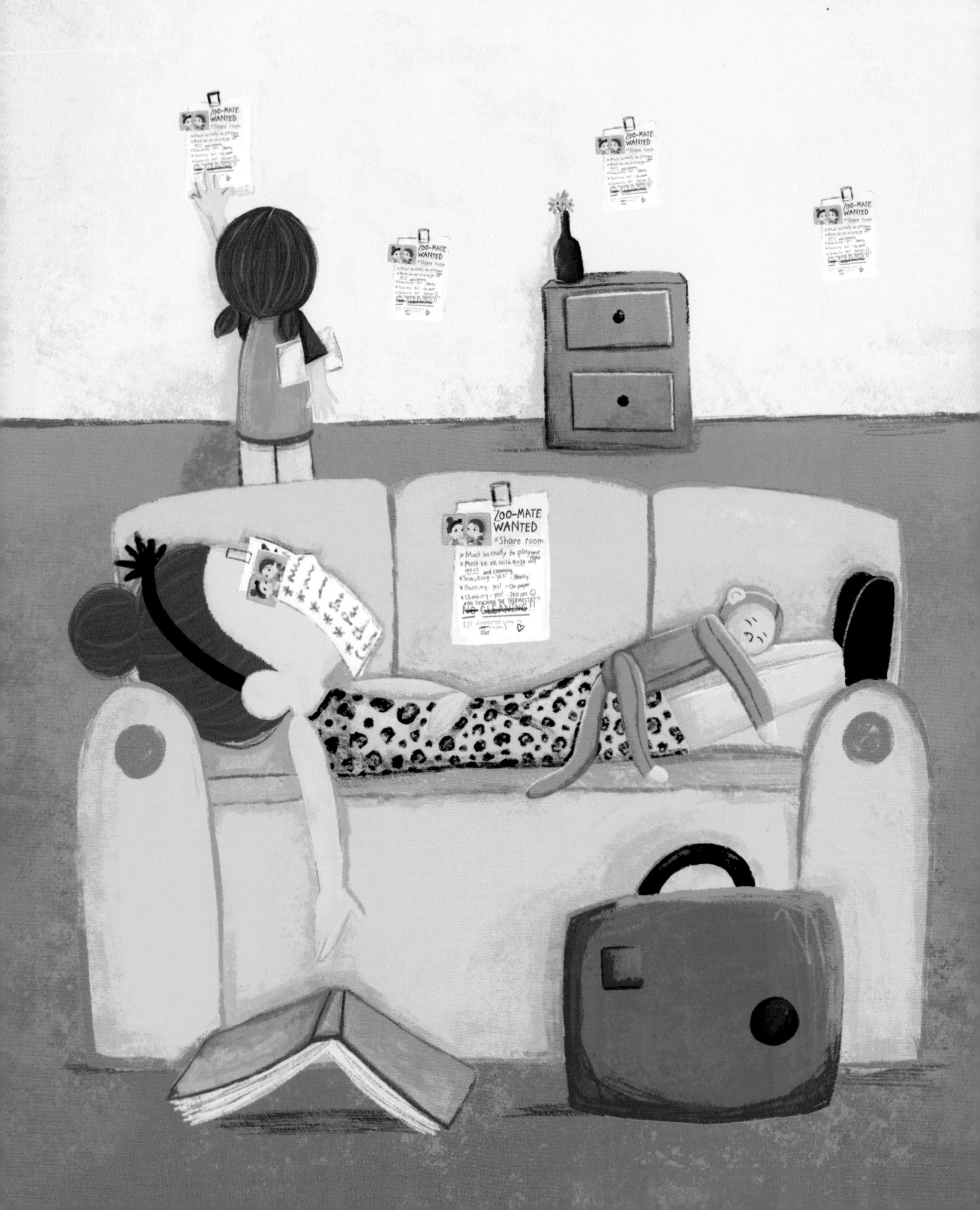

Finally...

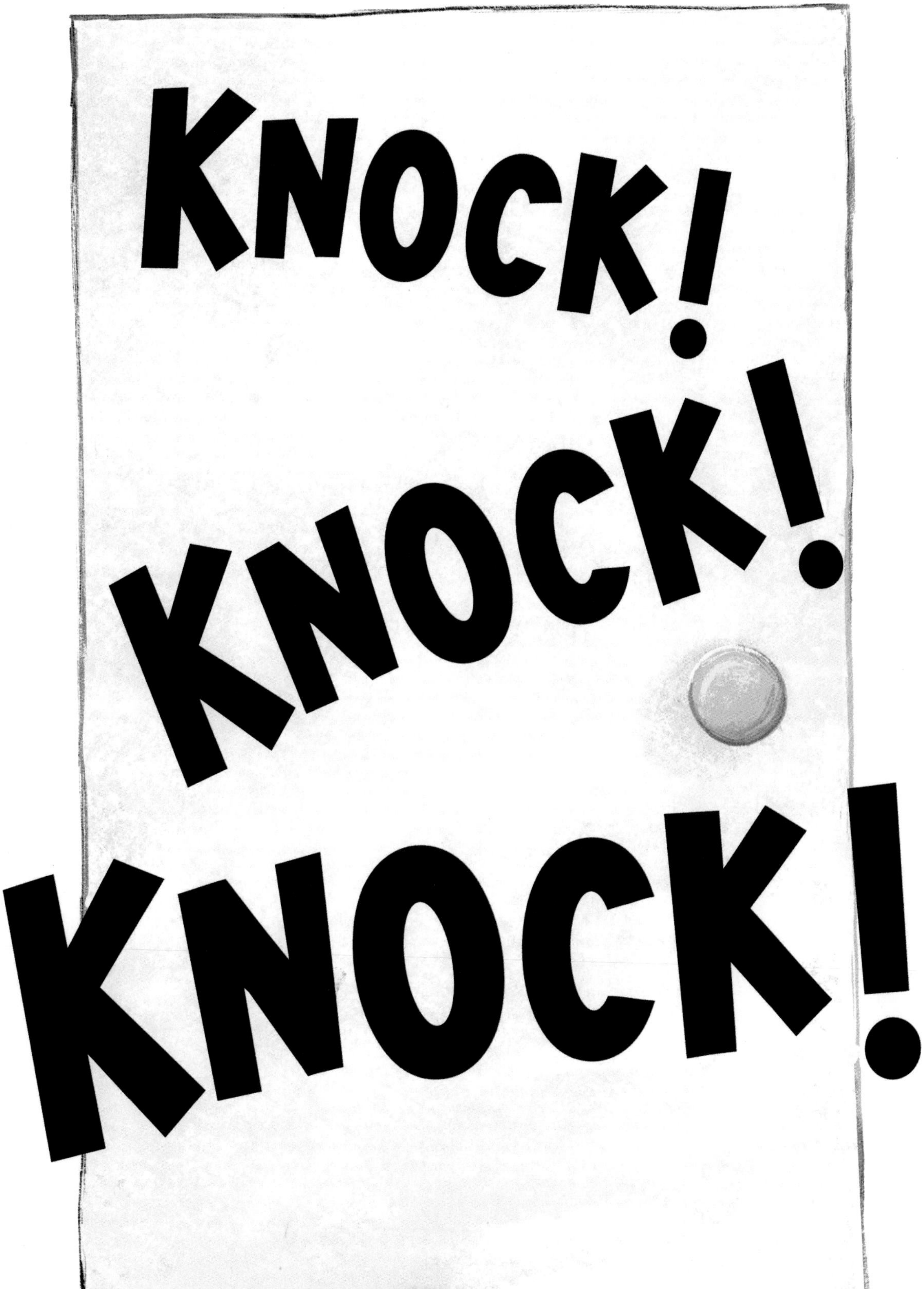

KNOCK!

KNOCK!

KNOCK!

"ABSOLUTELY YES!"

Some days, living together was still really hard.

But now Leah knew that having a zoo-mate was worth it.

Dedicated to Nate. My zoo-mate for life.—KL

Library of Congress Cataloging-in-Publication data is on file with the publisher.

First published in the United States of America in 2021 by Albert Whitman & Company
ISBN 978-0-8075-9565-7 (hardcover)
ISBN 978-0-8075-9568-8 (ebook)

Printed in China
10 9 8 7 6 5 4 3 2 1 WKT 24 23 22 21 20

For more information about Albert Whitman & Company,
visit our website at www.albertwhitman.com.